"Shimmering Dew"

A STORY OF FRIENDSHIP

Robert "Uti" Gebauer

"Shimmering Dew"

A STORY OF FRIENDSHIP

Copyright © 2022 by Robert "Uti" Gebauer. 841066

All rights reserved. No part of this book may be reproduced or transmitted in any form or by any means, electronic or mechanical, including photocopying, recording, or by any information storage and retrieval system, without permission in writing from the copyright owner.

This is a work of fiction. Names, characters, places and incidents either are the product of the author's imagination or are used fictitiously, and any resemblance to any actual persons, living or dead, events, or locales is entirely coincidental.

To order additional copies of this book, contact:
Xlibris
844-714-8691
www.Xlibris.com
Orders@Xlibris.com

ISBN:	Softcover	978-1-6698-2435-0
	Hardcover	978-1-6698-2436-7
	EBook	978-1-6698-2434-3

Library of Congress Control Number: 2022908609

Print information available on the last page

Rev. date: 05/10/2022

"Shimmering Dew"

“Shimmering Dew”

A story of friendship

By

Robert “Uti” Gebauer

On a remote island in the South Pacific, in one of the many tide pools along the beaches, a small starfish moves between the coral and sand. Her blue skin glistens like little twinkling stars under the water. Her arms are covered with tiny, hair-like feet, which she uses to move about, inching her way in the shallows of the tide pools.

It is early morning and the tide is low, a perfect time to explore the riches of the tide pool. The sun is up and shining its warm rays over the island and sea. Throughout the tide pools, many creatures are busy looking for food. Tiny fish are hiding under the rocks and larger fish are moving all around. Other creatures are just continuing with their daily lives.

High above the clouds, Fisaga the Wind God looks down upon this small island. He blows his cooling breeze over the island, and sees all the land and sea creatures carrying on with their daily routine.

However, one special starfish is not looking for food, instead she likes to reach out of the water and experience the warmth of the sun on her body. This is very hard for this sea creature because she is not able to breath outside of the water and she moves very slowly. Bravely, she has taught herself to hold her breath and then gently push her body out of the water for short periods.

Over time, she has managed to stay out of the water for no more than one minute and then she must return back into the ocean to take a breath. Her daily routine is to look for food then to continue with her air breathing practice. At the end of her day, she goes back to the coral reef under the water.

Unique to this starfish, are her 6 legs and not 5, which make her different from others of her kind. Many of the sea creatures see her as an outcast because of her extra limb and more because she is different. This does not stop this small and determined starfish. She labors at her daily routine and moves slowly in and out of the water trying to feel the warmth of the sun.

She lives alone and longs for friendship but none is near. So she continues with her routine and the cool breeze softly caresses her skin.

This starfish is called Taimane and she lives on the reef that surrounds the little island of Luamo'o. This island is special and home to many animals, especially migrating birds. Every now and then a new flock of birds come and then leave when their time is up to return to their homes. Unlike many of those birds that come to visit, Taimane's permant home is near this tiny island.

Every day, Taimane waits for the tides to change, especially to low tide, so she can quickly come out of the water and explore life above the sea. When she is above the sea she looks at some of the land creatures. She often sees many birds flying and coming to the shoreline to look for food; some birds try to catch her as their meal. But she manages to evade their capture.

Taimane has learned to stay in the deeper side of the tide pools when those birds are foraging. Although some birds may harm her, Taimane enjoys seeing life above the water and moves with the tide, in and out as the waves rush to the shore.

On some occasions, she would follow the sun during low tide and would push herself out of the water while holding her breath. She spends her days alone foraging for food and daydreaming. She then she returns back to the ocean. Some nights when the tides are right, she peeks out of the ocean to see the stars dancing in the sky.

Some nights when there is a full moon, Taimane would watch the moonlight shine through the water and she would dream of how it would be to live above the ocean; especially when she sees the moonbeams dance across the water, glistening with color as the waves move back and forth in the night. She often imagines these shimmering lights are her imaginary sea fairies and she dreams they are her friends, since she is always alone.

Occasionally she whispers to them to make her dream come true. “Oh pretty fairies, please grant me my wish.” Fisaga the Wind God often hears her prayers and softly whispers in the wind with a cooling breath.

As Taimane plays in the water, she persistently tries to stay out of the water for longer periods. Sadly the longer she stays out of the water, the more pain and weakness she feels. Her inability to breath above the ocean causes her to feel lightheaded and makes her sick.

To recover, she must return to the ocean and gain her strength. For the most part, she tries to stay above water only for short periods and rarely gets sick. Usually, she would hold her breath and then slowly inch her way above the water line and enjoy the feeling of air on her scales, but it never lasts, because she must return back into the sea.

Sadly, staying out of water causes her skin to dry and slowly peel. Constant exposure to the air causes her skin to flake and appear as shimmering dust. Although the dryness caused by the wind and air may be uncomfortable, the warmth of the sun makes her happy. So she continues her sun bathing as often as she can.

Over the years, she has gotten better, but at a terrible price. She can hold her breath just long enough to the reach the sand from the tide pool. She loves the feel of the sand on her body, soft and grainy. Warm to the touch. But these are very short visits and only possible as long as she can hold her breath.

The longer she stays above the ocean, the more dangerous her situation becomes. No matter how many times she tries to breathe air above the ocean, she is not able to draw a breath. All she feels is pain from gasping for air and must immediately return to the water for the breath of life.

Over time, the long exposure to air has wreaked havoc to her skin; it has become dry and has started to fall off. Sometimes when the sun is high and there is a breeze, a trail of her dried skin can be seen floating in the breeze. The trail reflects the sunshine and glimmers in the air.

On those rare occasions when she stays longer out of the water, she leaves a trail of flakes along the sand. Often these flakes would drift in the air and twinkle in the sunshine as the winds blow the particles in all directions. Fisaga is often sad when this trail of light flows high above the clouds.

One day, as Taimane was moving through the tide pools, she noticed a dark shadow hovering above her. This shadowy figure seemed to be trying to get her attention. As she moved left, it moved left, as she moves right, it followed. This confused poor Taimane because she had never known such a thing. Suddenly, taking a deep breath under the water, she peeked up and pulled herself out of the water. Looking down at her was a long beak and with big eyes.

Taimane was frightened and immediately retreated under the water. However, this shadowy figure continued to block the sun and continued to hover directly above her. Her instincts tell her to flee, but she was curious to know what is hovering above her. So she gathered up all her strength, took a deep breath and once again pulled herself above the water.

Shockingly, she hears a thundering voice exclaim, "Please do not go, I will not harm you." It was a pounding voice, deep and loud like thunder clanging.

Bravely, Taimane held her breath and opened her eyes and to see a huge land creature with long legs and a huge head. More importantly, the head had a very large yellow beak. Taimane was scared. The head also had large eyes, which were looking down at her from way above the water. This creature had green and red skin that moved in wind: it had feathers.

It was not a cloud but a land creature she had never seen before. The creature spoke again, "My name is Toalii and I am a Sea Crane. I just arrived to your island. I am traveling from a far away land and I wanted some place warm to rent."

Taimane was surprised and dropped back into the water to get a full breath before picking herself up again and blurted out in a very soft voice before grasping for air, " please do not eat me."

Toalii answered, "I will not eat you, I am just resting here in the tide pool. It is so hot today. I wanted to cool off."

Both started talking in their unique way. Taimane gasping and talking fast and Toalii talking above water while Taimane listened under the water. As the days turned into weeks and then months, Taimane and Toalii became very good friends. This was Taimane's first friend. Each low tide when the sun was high, Toalii would wait for Taimane and they would play and talk with each other.

Taimane would ask many questions of life above the ocean and Toalii would ask about life under the sea. Their talks would last until it was time for Taimane to return to the ocean and with each goodbye they both promised to see each other again the next day. Every time Taimane would leave to go back to the ocean, she would wish she were able to stay longer out of the water.

She had gotten better over the past few months, but she was still not able to stay out of the water entirely and her skin was showing signs of constant dryness. Lately, the constant strain to her body had begun to takes its toll. She was getting weaker from the exposure to the air above the ocean.

One day, Toalii waited to see his friend, but she never showed. Toalii returned every day for a week and still Taimane was nowhere to be seen. Then on the morning of the eighth day, Toalii saw his friend Taimane floating with the tide. She looked very weak and was not able to move on her own very well. The waves moved her up, down and sideways.

Toalii could tell she was not well. Toalii asked, “What is wrong Taimane?”

She responded very softly and apologized for not coming sooner and explained she was not able to visit because she had gotten weak from staying out of the ocean too often.

Toalii slowly picked her up softly with his beak and moved her to a shallow part of the beach, closer to where he could hear her soft voice but where the seawater could still cover her. The gentle waves kept her skin moist while she peaked out of the water in between breaths.

Toalii heard Taimane say in a trembling voice, "Toalii, I will be leaving you soon, please do not be sad. It is my time to go back into the ocean and not return, please remember me. Thank you for being my friend."

She also tells him that her one and only true dream was to find a friend. Her dream had come true. Toalii realizes his friend was very weak and felt responsible for her being sick.

Toalii answered sadly, "I will always remember you." Then he asked her if there was anything she wanted.

She replied, "I would like to feel the air and sun across my body high above the clouds where you fly."

Toalii sighed and nodded his head. Tears were falling upon the water and Taimane thought it had begun to rain. Toalii's orange feathers were moving in the wind as he nodded. His eyes were watery. As was her wish, Toalii picked up his tiny friend with his right claw and very tenderly flew swiftly above the clouds and as far as his wings would go. Toalii asked Taimane, as he got high above the clouds if she could feel the sun on her body, she nodded softly and then finally became still. Toalii knew his friend was gone.

He had been determined to fulfill her last wish and whispered to Taimane, "I will carry you high above the clouds," and whispered to himself. "I too had a wish. I always wanted a friend and it came true. You Taimane are my friend."

As he spoke he flew higher and higher till the air got so thin that he could not breathe. Then he took a huge gasp of air and flew higher still, until he could not fly any more.

As he looked back, he saw a trail of colors flowing over Taimane's body; yellow, green, blue and gold and they were twinkling in the air. Instantly, he recalled Taimane's pain when she tried to breath above the ocean. He was feeling that now, gasping for air.

He whispered, "I will always be with you, my friend." Then he gasped and took his last breath and they both began to fall from high above the clouds. As their bodies started falling, a trail of golden light flowed from Taimane's body reflecting the sun's golden hues. Magically, in midair, their bodies stopped falling and floated amongst the clouds.

What could have happened? As these friends bid their last goodbyes, Fisaga the wondering Wind God, had heard their farewells on the wind and was deeply touched by their sorrow, especially the sadness of their good byes.

Fisaga then motioned a bolt of lightning to strike where the bodies of the two friends were floating and a huge bolt clashed with a thundering bang. "KAPOOOOM!" It instantly transformed the two creatures into a shower of twinkling lights. Yellow, green, blue and gold were all dancing in the sky and then started to fall towards the ocean.

Fisaga did this as a memorial for two friends who cared for each other in spite of their differences and being alone. He did not want their sadness to be in vain. Instead, the Wind God turned their bodies into shimmering dew that would memorialize their friendship for all time.

Sometimes if you are lucky and if the Wind God is nearby, you might see a glimpse of Taimane and Toalii playing on the ocean. At other times, you will see the twinkling of lights upon the ocean before sunset. This is a memorial to two friends who overcame their hardships and who are forever together.

As the sun sets on those special days, you may see this special shimmering dew of light that glimmers in blue, green, yellow and gold over the water. They are forever sparkling and forever together. They are no longer alone.

The End.

Printed in the United States
by Baker & Taylor Publisher Services

Printed in the United States
by Baker & Taylor Publisher Services